# I WANT TO BE FREE

by
**JOSEPH SLATE**

*illustrated by*
**E. B. LEWIS**

G. P. PUTNAM'S SONS

G. P. PUTNAM'S SONS

A division of Penguin Young Readers Group.

Published by The Penguin Group. Penguin Group (USA) Inc., 375 Hudson Street, New York, NY 10014, U.S.A. Penguin Group (Canada), 90 Eglinton Avenue East, Suite 700, Toronto, Ontario M4P 2Y3, Canada (a division of Pearson Penguin Canada Inc.). Penguin Books Ltd, 80 Strand, London WC2R 0RL, England. Penguin Ireland, 25 St. Stephen's Green, Dublin 2, Ireland (a division of Penguin Books Ltd.). Penguin Group (Australia), 250 Camberwell Road, Camberwell, Victoria 3124, Australia (a division of Pearson Australia Group Pty Ltd). Penguin Books India Pvt Ltd, 11 Community Centre, Panchsheel Park, New Delhi - 110 017, India. Penguin Group (NZ), 67 Apollo Drive, Rosedale, North Shore 0632, New Zealand (a division of Pearson New Zealand Ltd). Penguin Books (South Africa) (Pty) Ltd, 24 Sturdee Avenue, Rosebank, Johannesburg 2196, South Africa. Penguin Books Ltd, Registered Offices: 80 Strand, London WC2R 0RL, England.

Design by Richard Amari.
Text set in ITC Cushing.
The art was done in watercolor on paper.

Library of Congress Cataloging-in-Publication Data
Slate, Joseph. I want to be free / Joseph Slate; illustrated by E. B. Lewis. p. cm. Summary: Based on a sacred Buddist tale as related in Rudyard Kipling's novel "Kim," tells of an escaped slave who rescues an abandoned baby from slave hunters. [1. Slaves—Fiction. 2. Slavery—Fiction. 3. Stories in rhyme.] I. Lewis, Earl B., ill. II. Title.
PZ8.3.S629Be 2009 [E]—dc22 2007038356
ISBN 978-0-399-24342-4
1 3 5 7 9 10 8 6 4 2

*For Patty,*

*who keeps me free.*

J. S.


*To the students and staff at the Hammond School.*

*Thanks for everything.*

E. B. L.

Before I die, I want to be free.
But the Big Man says, "You belong to me."

I try to run. I want to be free.
But they drag me back. And here I be.

He takes a ring. Clamps me round.
Gets up a chain. Binds me down.

Big Man's whip whistles with fear.
But I hear one tune: run, run from here.

I break the chain. I have no key.
Can't force the ring. It won't come free.

I hobble off. And while I run,
I thank the Lord He's banked the sun.

*Before I die, I want to be free.*
*But the Big Man says, "You belong to me."*

I find the camp of gone-free men.
They glad for me, but it ain't the end.

Big Man has dogs. He has a gun.
So we gather gear. Get ready to run.

They work at the ring, but it's no use.
It's Devil made. It won't pry loose.

*Before I die, I want to be free.*
*But the Big Man says, "You belong to me."*

Down deep in a bush, I hear this cryin'.
It's a little child close to dyin'.

I pick him up, but the others say,
"His mother's dead. He has to stay."

"Let the Big Man come. Take him back.
He has the farm. Food we lack."

"Oh no," says I. "We'll run to the wild!
The Lord will help me care for this child."

*Before I die, I want to be free.*
*But the Big Man says, "You belong to me."*

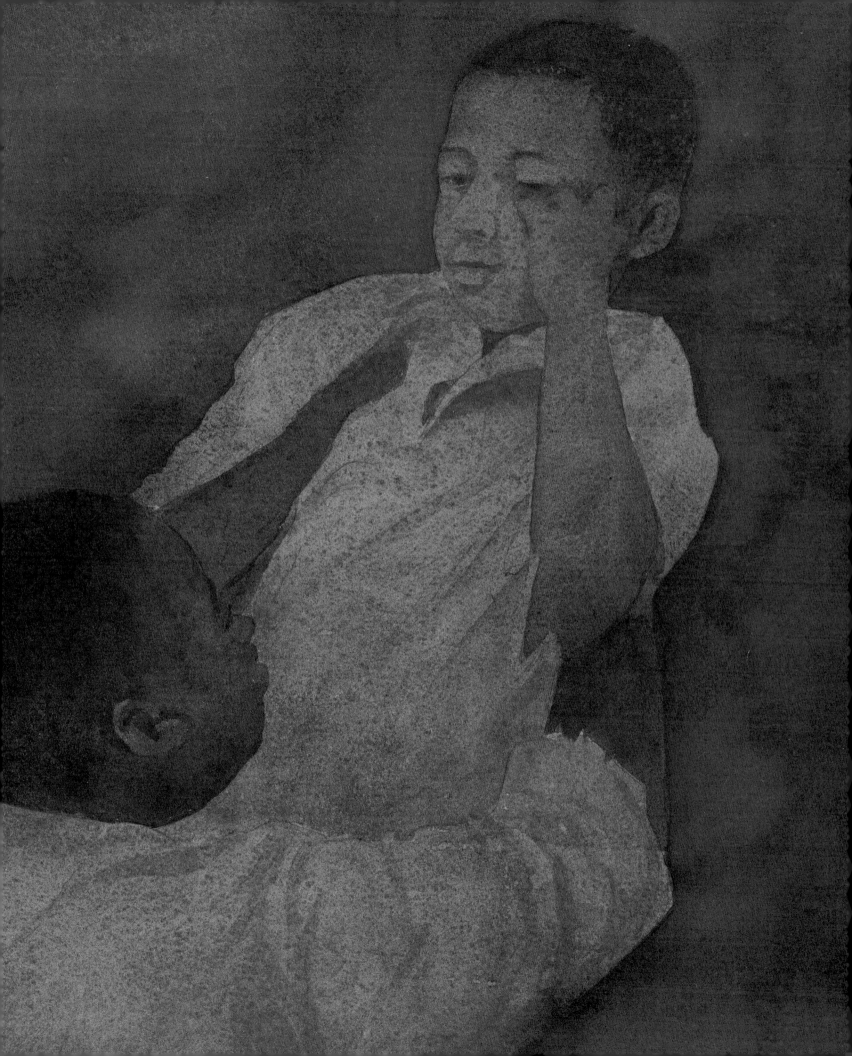

I take cow's milk. I gather fuel.
I take field corn to make us gruel.

The ring burned fearsome. It scoured my skin.
But there was no way I was gonna give in.

And that's how we got to the Land of the Free.
But the ring was still a sorrow to me.

One day, my child looked close at the ring.
Said, "Papa, Papa, what is that thing?"

I told him the story of that dark, dark day.

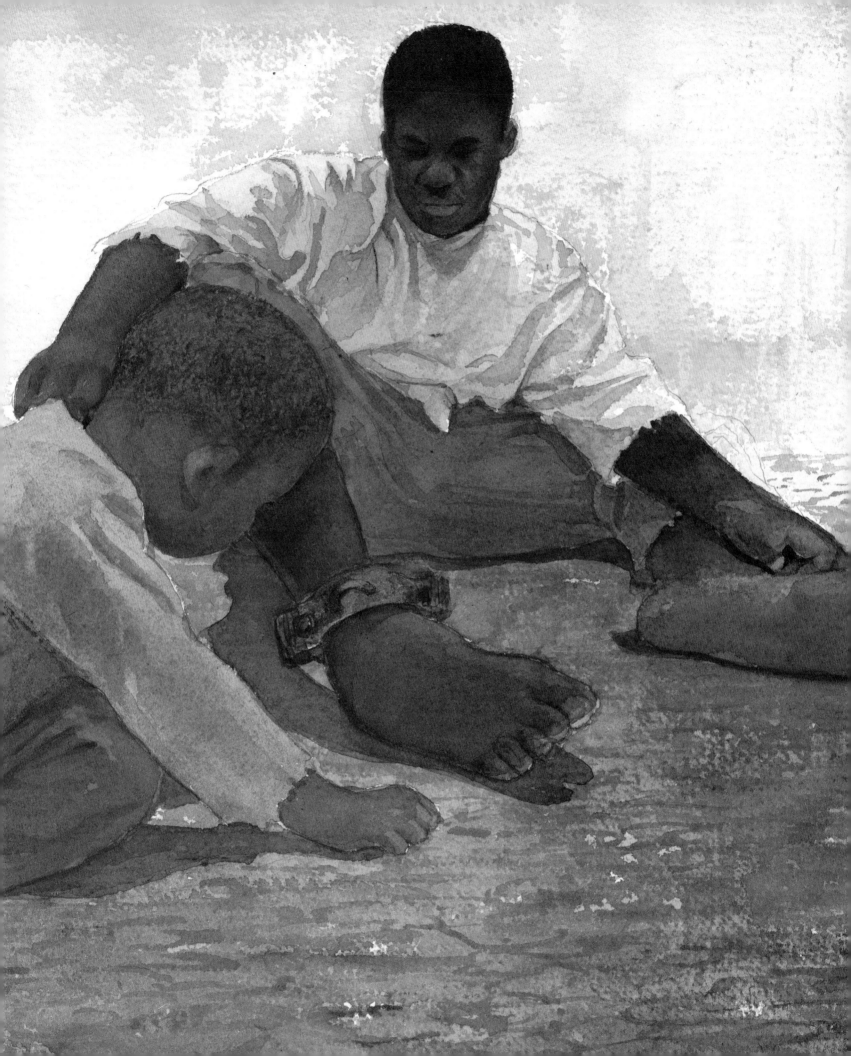

He touched the ring. It fell away.

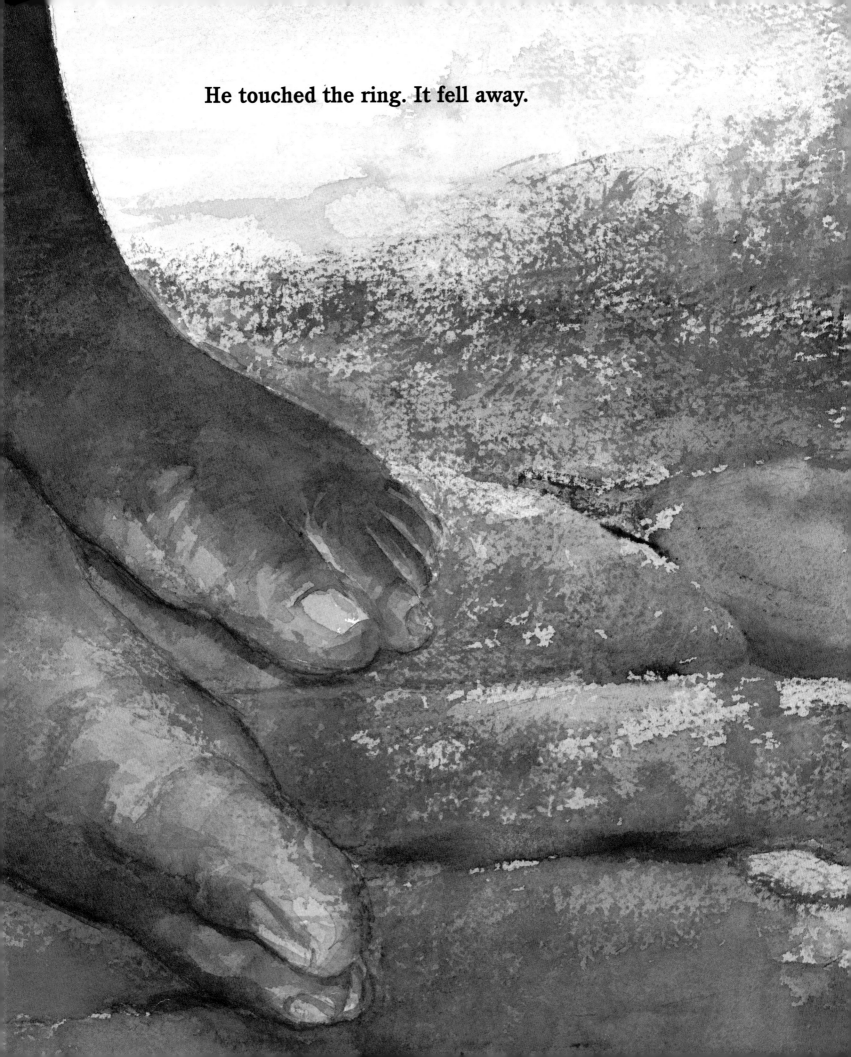

Tears welled up. Fell down my face.
I saw my child lit up by grace.

*"How, dear child, did you set me free?"*
*"I'm from the Lord. You cared for me."*

## AUTHOR'S NOTE

*This poem is a retelling of a story in the sacred literature of Buddha about his disciple, the Elephant Ananda, as related by Rudyard Kipling in his novel* Kim. *I moved its setting and language to another time, as I believe its themes to be universal.*

### J. S.

## ILLUSTRATOR'S NOTE

*Not only does* I Want To Be Free *tell a heroic story of the thirst for freedom by young people in the time of slavery, but it took me through an experience that I had not previously encountered. While doing my research, I decided to use Kentucky and Ohio as the geographical references. I had made the journey from Kentucky to one of the Underground Railroad safe places across the Ohio River before, but this time, while crossing the river, I imagined the dark nights when lives quietly swept across to the other side in a deeper way. I toured the Rankin House in Ripley, Ohio for the first time and stood still for a while to reflect on the risky and humane actions that helped free slaves during those times.*

*The spirit of this book has inspired me to further research slave narratives, safe houses, and the children who bravely and miraculously continue to shape all of our futures today.*

### E.B.L.